UP NORTH IN WINTER

That old fox just might have saved Grandpa's life, my Dad says.

Life's funny like that, I always say.
It sure gets cold up North in winter.

50475

JP
Hartley, Deborah.
Up north in winter $11.95

UP NORTH IN WINTER

by Deborah Hartley · illustrated by Lydia Dabcovich

E. P. DUTTON   NEW YORK

Library of Congress Cataloging-in-Publication Data
Hartley, Deborah.
    Up north in winter.
    Summary: A tale of a winter many years ago, in
which Grandpa carries home a fox and gets a surprise.
    [1. Winter—Fiction.   2. Grandfathers—Fiction.
3. Foxes—Fiction]   I. Dabcovich, Lydia, ill.
II. Title.
PZ7.H264Up   1986   [E]   86-4543
ISBN 0-525-44268-5

Published in the United States by E. P. Dutton,
2 Park Avenue, New York, N.Y. 10016

Published simultaneously in Canada by
Fitzhenry & Whiteside Limited, Toronto

Editor: Ann Durell   Designer: Riki Levinson

Printed in Hong Kong by South China Printing Co.
First Edition   COBE   10 9 8 7 6 5 4 3 2 1

to Erin and Patrick
D.H.

to Riki, who knows why
L.D.

It gets cold up North in winter.
Some nights it's so cold
folks could freeze to death, my Dad says.

My Grandpa Ole lived up North
a long time ago
when my father was a little boy like me.

Times were hard back then.
Grandpa didn't have very much money.
He worked all day, from sunrise to sunset,
to earn only one dollar for his family.
Hard work never hurt a man, my Dad says.

The winter of 1911 was the worst.
Grandma cooked mostly deer meat, rabbit,
potato soup and kale.

When Grandma's cow, Snow White, stopped giving milk,
even that old cow ended up in the soup pot.
Folks have to eat to live, my Dad says.

There was no work nearby that winter,
so Grandpa took a job in another town.
He rode the train there every Sunday night
and rode it back home on Friday evening.
A man has to find work where he can, my Dad says.

One Friday Grandpa worked late.
When he got to the station, the train had gone.

The night was icy cold.
Home was twelve miles away following the road;
cutting across the lake made it only six.
Grandpa headed for the lake.

He put his sack of clothes over his shoulder
and lit up his pipe. In the distance,
he could see the lights of his own town—
about a three-hour walk away.
Then he started across the frozen lake.

Halfway home, dog tired and pretty near frozen himself,
Grandpa stumbled over something on the ice.
He looked down to see a big fox lying there
dead—but still warm.

My Grandpa knew he could get ten dollars
for a prime fox pelt. He would have to work
two weeks for that much money.
Grandpa's heart started pounding hard.
Sometimes a man just gets lucky, my Dad says.

Grandpa stuffed his pipe in his pocket,
picked up that fox, and wrapped it around his shoulders
to protect himself from the wind.

Finding that fox gave Grandpa new energy.
Now he walked on much faster through the icy night.
He smiled to himself.
Ten dollars would sure help fill up those bare pantry shelves.

Grandpa finally reached his home.
Shivering and exhausted, he set the fox down
outside the door.

He thought how worried Grandma must be
with him being so late.
He could just imagine the look on her face
as he showed her his prize.
He gave a knock.

Grandma opened the door...

and at that very moment the fox jumped up and
shot off like a cannonball across the yard.
That fox wasn't dead.
It had just been too cold to move.

Grandma said she was thankful
the excitement of finding the fox
brought Grandpa home safely
on such a bitter cold night.